THE TALE OF
TWM SIÔN CATI

by

Margaret Isaac

Illustrations by

Margaret Jones

APECS PRESS △ CAERLEON

Published by
APECS Press
Caerleon
Wales UK

Editing and design by
APECS Press Caerleon

ISBN 0 9548940 1 4

Printed in Wales by Gwasg Dinefwr Llandybie

CONTENTS

By the same author

Tales of Gold: Stories of Caves, Gold and Magic.

Nia and the Magic of the Lake: The story of a growing friendship between a boy and a girl set against the backdrop of the legend of Llyn-y-Fan Fach

Sir Gawain and the Green Knight: It is Christmas time in King Arthur's court. Gawain, Arthur's nephew, accepts a mortal challenge from an enchanted giant.

Rhiannon's Way: Caradog, a Celtic chieftain, has been captured by the Romans. His daughter Rhiannon sets out to rescue him with the help of her friend Brychan and a little help from a magic pony and a magic mirror.

Teaching Story in the Primary School (1)
(Language resources for Key Stage 1 based on the story 'The Owl Who Was Afraid of the Dark' by Jill Tomlinson).

Language Learning through Story (1)
(Language resources for Key Stage 2 based on the story 'Tales of Gold' by Margaret Isaac).

Language Learning through Story (2)
(Language resources for Key Stage 2 based on the story 'Nia and the Magic of the Lake' by Margaret Isaac).

Language Learning through Story (3)
(Language resources for Key Stage 2 based on the story 'Sir Gawain and the Green Knight' translated by Margaret Isaac).

Forthcoming publications

Language Learning through story (4)
(Language resources for Key Stage 2 based on the story 'Rhiannon's Way' by Margaret Isaac).

Language Learning through story (5)
(Language resources for Key Stage 2 based on the story 'The Tale of Twm Siôn Cati' by Margaret Isaac).

Lake Legends of Wales
A series of short stories based on traditional tales.

A NOTE ABOUT
THOMAS JONES: TWM SIÔN CATI

MORE THAN 450 years ago, around the year 1530 to be more exact, a baby boy was born to a pretty peasant girl called Catherine, known locally as Cati. The boy was christened Thomas, his full name was Thomas Jones, but he was also sometimes known as Tomas Siôn Dafydd Madoc. The name itself is ordinary, but this baby was most extraordinary, for he grew up to become the notorious outlaw known as Twm Siôn Cati. His birthplace was Porth y Ffynnon (Fountain Gate) near Tregaron, a village some twenty miles from Aberystwyth in Mid-Wales.

In the days when Twm was born, the life of a peasant was very hard, the ordinary Welsh people were downtrodden by harsh and unjust laws. Folk scratched a living from the land, or worked as lead miners deep in the earth. Some may have worked in the gold mines, but the gold would have been claimed by the wealthy landowners who employed them. Thieves were hanged, sometimes for stealing a loaf of bread to feed their starving families, and their bodies would be left on gibbets as a warning to others. People were pinioned in the stocks for not doffing their caps to the vicar, for even vicars in those days could be cruel and unjust.

In these times of poverty and persecution, Twm Siôn Cati carried out many bold deeds to help his people. They, in turn, were proud of their hero and often aided him when he embarked on his daring adventures. Of course the squires who persecuted the common folk hated Twm Siôn Cati and did their utmost to capture him, but he was clever as well as brave and usually outwitted them. He had the strength of a lion, but he was better known for his clever disguises and his gift of mimicry.

Despite his mischievous ways, he was himself a man of noble blood and became a respected antiquary, genealogist and poet. His father was Siôn ap Dafyddd ap Madog ap Hywel Moetheu. Catherine's father, Twm's grandfather, Maredydd ap Ieuan ap Robert, was also related to some of the highest ranking families of Wales. Because of this relationship with the Welsh aristocracy and because Twm Siôn Cati felt keenly the persecution of his people, he vowed that, one day, he would be respected in all the land.

The story about to unfold is one of a hero who survives against all the odds. He dupes the powerful squire Jasper Tyler and the cruel, greedy shop keeper Elias. In doing so he risks his life.

So *The Tale of Twm Siôn Cati* is a tale of mischief and adventure, of greed and danger, of love, laughter and courage. It is the story of a man who learns to survive against the greatest odds and who lives to become one of the most respected Welshmen of his time. He died in the year 1609.

TWM IS BORN

A THIN WISP of smoke curled upwards to the sky from a house in Tregaron. Inside, women busied themselves around the baby's cot and attended to the new mother. Outside, a Red Kite hovered on the wing. A small rabbit cowered in the long thin grass below. The bird swooped, the rabbit screeched as the new born baby cried.

Miriam, the midwife, carefully cleaned the tiny mouth, nose and eyes.

'What a beautiful child,' cried Elisabeth, 'a healthy baby boy.' She smiled at the bundle cradled in Miriam's arms. The midwife carefully placed the child in the wooden cot at the foot of the bed. She moved to attend to the young mother.

'She's exhausted, poor love,' she said.

'How will she look after the child?' said Elisabeth, 'she's just a strip of a lass herself.'

Elisabeth was a young girl of about sixteen years of age. She lived in a small cottage near Porth y Ffynnon or Fountain Gate as it was known in English in Tregaron, and had known Cati all her life.

'How old is she?' asked Miriam. Miriam was the local midwife and did not know Cati as well as Elisabeth.

'She's just fourteen,' said Anne, Cati's mother, 'and we'll look after her, Maredydd and me'. She was sitting quietly in the corner of the bedroom.

'Has anyone told the baby's father?' whispered Miriam.

'I've told Gruffydd to ride over to Dinefwr,' Elizabeth replied. Gruffydd was her sweetheart. 'He should be told, he is the father after all.' As she spoke, the door of the bedroom opened and Gwyneth appeared with a bowl of steaming broth. Gwyneth, a young girl of fourteen, was Elisabeth's cousin. Cati stirred and opened her eyes. She was immediately anxious.

'Where's my baby,' she whispered.

'He's fine,' said Miriam soothingly, 'You have a lovely baby boy.'

'Let me see him,' said Cati. Miriam handed

the baby carefully to his young mother. Cati cradled her child in her arms. The baby kicked its legs and snuggled up to Cati's breast, its eyes shut, its eyelids a lovely pale violet colour. Cati looked at the baby's face.

'Hello my lovely,' she crooned, 'we'll have great times together you and me, I promise you.'

'Let me have him Cati,' said Miriam, 'while you eat this lovely broth, I've brought you. You need to keep your strength up.'

'What will you call him, Cati?' asked Elisabeth.

'Twm,' said Cati, without hesitation. She mused . . .' and . . . Siôn, after my cousin, John Wyn.' The women looked at each other. Cousin was a loose term of family associations. They had heard rumours that the child's natural father was connected with the rich and powerful Moethu family and had bestowed on Cati the house she lived in, Fountain Gate. Only Cati knew the truth.

'And Cati, after you,' laughed Elisabeth.

And so Twm Siôn Cati was born.

CATI
THE SCHOOLTEACHER

1T WAS A LOVELY Spring Day. Daffodils were swaying in soft March breezes, sheep were placidly munching on the green hillside. Cati and her son Twm had lived at Fountain Gate from the time he was born. She lived there with her mother Anne, and her father Maredydd.

As her friend Elizabeth walked down the street of Tregaron, she heard Cati's voice as it floated through the open window at Fountain Gate. She was singing an old Welsh song:

Oes gafr eto . . .

A man's voice joined in,

Oes heb ei godro . . .

Soon father and daughter were singing the song together while Twm, her son, danced round the kitchen table clapping his hands in time to the music.

'I could do with some help in the kitchen,' a

woman's voice shouted to Cati and Maredydd, her father.

'Coming Mam,' said Cati, and joined her mother. They started placing the plates and food on the table.

'What's for breakfast Mam?' asked Twm. He was a fine fellow of five years, with dark curly hair and large brown eyes.

'A lovely brown egg, bread, butter and a mug of milk,' replied his mother. Cati and her mother and father sat at the table with Twm, enjoying the first meal of the day.

A knock came at the door and Cati called out, 'Come in.' Elizabeth, Cati's friend, opened the door and came in to the kitchen. She sat companionably at the table.

'I heard the singing and thought I'd pop in to see how you were,' she said.

'Have you had your breakfast?' asked Cati's mother.

'Yes, thank you,' replied Elizabeth. 'I just came in for a chat.' She watched with amusement as the yolk of the egg dribbled down Twm's chin. Cati cleaned him up and carried on with her own meal. Twm smiled winningly at Elizabeth.

'I was talking to Gwenllian Cadwgan this morning,' said Elizabeth. 'She is so angry with Vicar Griffiths and his wife. Gwenllian's two little ones, Gwendolen and Rhys, came home yesterday with black and blue weals on the backs of their legs from the beating they had from the vicar's wife, just because they could not say their letters.' Anne sat with her elbows on the table, her mug of ale untouched.

'Lots of people round here don't like the way they run their school,' she said. 'They are so strict, and punish the children over the smallest thing: and they charge too much. People can't afford to send their children to the school every day, but they want them to be able to read and write so that they won't have to end up working in the fields like their fathers or skivvying for the rich folk like their mothers.'

'You read and write beautifully Cati,' said Elizabeth. 'When we were in the same class in the church school, I remember you were always better at your letters than the rest of us. And you've always had a marvellous memory, you tell so many fabulous stories and sing such beautiful songs.'

'I learned those from my parents and my grandparents,' laughed Cati, 'the vicar wouldn't know most of them. But I suppose I was good at my letters, I do like reading and writing, but I did find that church catechism boring.'

'You were pretty good at counting too,' said Elizabeth. She admired her friend very much and always enjoyed her lively company. 'You would make an extremely interesting schoolteacher, if you had a mind to it.'

'I don't know,' mused Cati, 'I don't think I would be very good at making them behave, I don't behave all that well myself come to that.' She laughed again, as she looked at her son and ruffled his hair affectionately.

'That's not a bad thing.' Maredydd, her father, spoke for the first time. He was usually a quiet man, and had been listening intently to the women's conversation.

'Maybe children would enjoy their lessons a bit more if they had you to teach them.' He went on thoughtfully, 'Children learn better if they are enjoying what they are learning. However, the Vicar wouldn't like you setting up a school, you would take away his pupils and his money.'

'That doesn't bother me,' said Cati, 'I don't

care much for his church ways, it doesn't seem all that Christian, beating children to make them learn their lessons. Besides I could do with some extra money.'

'You've got a splendid large house, here at Fountain Gate,' said her mother. 'You could use the big front room for your schoolroom. It would be beautifully light with the sun streaming in through the windows, why not give it a try?'

'I'll think about it,' said Cati.

Next day, Twm came home looking red faced and crestfallen.

'What's the matter?' asked Cati, anxiously.

'I couldn't say my letters and Mrs Griffiths smacked me.' His face was tearstained, but he looked defiant and angry.

'Where did she hit you? Let me see,' said his mother. Twm turned round and showed the back of his legs. Two angry looking black and blue weals showed up just below his knees.

'That's it,' said Cati angrily, 'I shall start my own school tomorrow.' She went out into the garden and chose a large stout stick. Twm watched anxiously, he knew his mother had a quick temper.

'You are not going to take that down to the vicar's school are you?' he asked. He thought his mother might be thinking of giving the vicar's wife a taste of her own medicine. But Cati only took the stick into the house and laid it on the floor of the kitchen.

She took out of a drawer a large piece of parchment, some ink and a quill pen. She sat at her desk writing carefully on a large piece of parchment.

Cati tied the notice to the stick and, taking Twm by the hand, she walked out of Fountain Gate and down the road through the village. She was soon joined by a band of children. Mothers and fathers came out into the street to see what was going on.

'That's not a bad idea,' said one of the mothers, 'my little boy's legs were black and blue when he came home yesterday. Cati can read and write, why not give her a try?'

**NEW SCHOOL OPENING
AT FOUNTAIN GATE**

LESSONS GIVEN IN READING,
WRITING AND COUNTING

BY CATI, DAUGHTER OF
MAREDYDD AP IEUAN AP ROBERT

ALSO MUSIC, GAMES AND DANCING

STORIES TOLD EVERY DAY

NO CHILD WILL BE BEATEN
FOR NOT KNOWING HIS LETTERS

SCHOOL STARTS AT 9 O'CLOCK
AND ENDS AT 3 O'CLOCK

FREE DINNERS

The mothers and fathers nodded thoughtfully as they returned to their homes.

FIRST DAY
IN CATI'S SCHOOL

THE SUN STREAMED through the windows of the big room in Fountain Gate. Four boys and four girls, aged between five and seven years of age, sat on wooden seats, their slates on their laps, hornbooks hanging from their wrists or waists. Cati sat on the big seat in front of the children, her elbows on the lid of the desk, her face intent, as she listened to Watt reading from his horn book.

In those days, children were taught to read by learning first of all to count the syllables in a word. In Watt's hornbook, the syllables were broken up inside the word to help the children to count them. Watt began reading:

'What let-ters make one syl-la-ble?' His finger wandered across the parchment on his hornbook as he tried to read the words. Watt continued,

'Any of the vowels, a,e,i,o,u, as you will find in

the words a-ny, e-vill, i-dle, o-ver-tur-neth, u-ni-ty.' Watt stopped, he looked puzzled,

'I don't know what that means Cati,' he said, as he looked longingly at the sunshine streaming through the window.

'I don't know if I do either,' said Cati, she sighed, 'some old cant from the vicar's school, I expect. Well, leave that for now. Turn your hornbooks over children.' They did so obediently. On the other side of the hornbook, the words of the Lord's Prayer were written.

'Say the words after me,' said Cati. Her voice was as persuasive as she could make it.

She began:

'O-U-R F-A-T-H-E-R W-H-O A-R-T I-N H-E-A-V-E-N.'

The children recited the words after her in a deadly monotone. One or two of the younger ones started to fidget.

Watt looked at Twm, who was sitting next to him, but his friend was staring out of the window. He looked across at Gwenni, she was playing with the hair ribbons in her plaits and looked bored He pushed the hornbook on to the desk in front of him.

'I don't understand this either,' said Watt plaintively, 'and I'm so hot, can't we go out to play, Cati?' Watt's voice was also persuasive.

Cati looked through the window at the cool green grass beneath the fruit trees in her garden. She looked again at the children sitting in front of her, their horn books on their laps. They looked flushed and hot.

'I think we would all be better for a spell outside in the garden. Come on children, let's all get a little fresh air and play a few games. Then we'll come back in the schoolroom for a few more lessons.'

The children gave a whoop of joy and rushed out of the school and down to the end of the garden.

'Let's play hide and seek!' said Gwendolen to her friends Jane and Megan.

'Alright,' said Jane, 'but you are IT.'

'Right,' said Gwendolen.

So they tied a scarf round Gwendolen's eyes and turned her round. Then the girls ran away while she counted.

'1, 2, 3, 4, 5, 6, 7, 8, 9, 10, ready or not I'm coming!' Gwendolen pulled the scarf from her eyes and looked round, listening carefully. She began to move round the garden. She thought she heard a sound coming from Cati's pigsty and crept quietly in that direction. Jane and Megan smothered a giggle.

Meanwhile, Twm, Watt, Owen, and Rhys were playing tug-of-war. But Twm noticed Gwendolen creeping towards the pigsty and had an idea.

'Come with me boys,' he said and led them into his mother's house. He searched out the box where Cati kept all the costumes for the May Day dances and the Mari Lwyd.

'This is good,' cried Twm as he held up a mask. 'Let's find some masks and give the girls a fright!'

In the meantime, Gwendolen crept closer to where her friends were hiding. Suddenly she gave a scream as a head appeared from behind an old pear tree near the pigsty, it was covered with the mask of a horse's skull.

'I'll get you now Gwendolen,' threatened a deep voice from inside the skull mask. Gwenni, Jane and Megan ran screaming to Cati who was sitting on a swing under the apple tree, enjoying the coolness of the shade.

'Cati! Cati! there's a . . . creature . . . down by the pigsty.' Cati jumped out of the swing and ran down to the pigsty with the girls only to find

Twm, Watt, Owen and Rhys rolling about on the ground, laughing fit to burst. Twm held the skull mask in his hand.

'Get up at once,' said Cati angrily, 'it's no laughing matter frightening the girls like that. If that's the way you behave, we'll have no more games, instead we'll have nothing but lessons all day in the schoolroom. Go and sit on the grass in front of the window,' she ordered.

The children sat in front of Cati on the grass. Cati sat in the shade of the tree on a stool. The girls' eyes were red with weeping and they looked quite sad. The boys were very crestfallen.

Cati did not believe in punishing children with a stick as they did in the vicar's school. But she wanted to show Twm that he had been wrong to make Gwenni, Jane and Megan cry. He was still very young but she wanted him to grow up to be kind to his friends. Cati looked at her young pupils and began,

'I'm going to tell you a story, about a kind man who became very unkind. His name was Morgan. He was a poor farmer who lived in this village a long time ago. The story is called:

MORGAN
AND THE FAIRIES

One dark night, there was a knock at Morgan's door. When he opened the door he saw three travellers.

'Can you give us food and shelter for the night,' they said. 'We have travelled far and are very weary.'

'Certainly,' said Morgan, who was a very kind man.

The three travellers came in to Morgan's house and he gave them a hot supper and a warm comfortable bed for the night. In the morning, as the three travellers prepared to depart, they said to him:

'We are not what we seem, Morgan. We are pleased that you showed so much kindness to three strangers and we would like to give you something in return. We will grant you one wish.' Morgan thought for a little and said:

'I have always longed for a harp. I love to play and I like music and dancing but I have never had enough money to buy a harp. I would have much pleasure playing to my family and friends.'

'Your wish is granted,' said the travellers and they disappeared. To his astonishment Morgan saw, where they had been standing, a beautiful harp. He picked it up and plucked the strings lovingly. The harp made the most beautiful music.

That night he invited his friends to his house for an evening's entertainment and he started to play his harp. The friends began to dance to the music, but they found that as long as Morgan played the harp they were forced to keep on dancing.

'Stop! Stop!' they cried, but Morgan began to laugh at his friends as they danced and cavorted around the kitchen. He thought it was a great joke to play his harp and make them keep on dancing, although they kept begging him to stop. Morgan realised that the harp was enchanted, and that his friends were forced to keep on dancing until he decided to stop playing. When he grew tired of watching his friends forced to dance by this enchanted music, he finally decided that he had played enough. He rested his fingers on the strings and placed the harp on the floor by his side.

His friends were so exhausted, they collapsed in a heap on to the floor. As they slowly regained enough strength to stand up and make their way towards the door of Morgan's house, they turned to him and cried angrily,

'We won't be coming to your house again in a hurry. You have always been kind and gentle, but that harp has changed you into a cruel monster. Play your music when you like, you won't have any company to enjoy it with you'. They really were very angry with Morgan and can you blame them?

Although Morgan was upset by his friends' words, he was so enchanted with his magic harp that he ignored them and went on playing his music. In fact, he sat near his window and when he saw the village people pass by he immediately picked up his harp and started to play, So anyone passing by were forced to dance, even if they were old or if they were unable to walk very well. When he saw them cavorting to the music, he only laughed louder and thought they looked funny as they danced away to the magic harp. They begged him to stop, but he laughed as he saw them jumping about, and cried out loudly,

'Serve you right for treating me so unkindly when I invited you to my home.' Morgan had changed from being a kind man to being very unkind to his friends and neighbours. He laughed and laughed at them, and kept on playing his music, making the villagers dance to his tune.

Then, one day, he got up in the morning and went to the corner where he kept his harp so that he could play it again and to his astonishment he found that the magic instrument had completely disappeared! The three fairies (for that was who the travellers were), had decided to take away the gift they had given to Morgan for his kindness to them, because they could see that he had become unkind to his friends and neighbours.

Morgan was very sad, but he never saw his harp or the three travellers again.'

Cati ended her story.

Gwendolen looked at Twm and Watt. Twm looked a little crestfallen. Then he saw Gwenni smile at him. She was a very forgiving child.

'Come on Twm,' she said. 'I'll race you back to the classroom.'

Cati came in from the garden and sat in front of the children with her harp in front of her.

'Right, girls and boys,' she said with a smile, 'I promise you that this is not like Morgan's harp. Let's end the morning with a singing lesson. I've prepared some bread and cheese and apples and some mugs of ale. When we have finished singing, you can have your dinner and I'll let you go home early since it is your first day. But I hope I will see you all again early tomorrow morning.'

So the children sang their songs, Cati played her harp and they all went home well fed and contented.

'How was your first day in Cati's school?' asked Gwendolen's mother.

'It was wonderful,' said Gwendolen. 'Can I go again tomorrow please?'

TWM PLAYS
A TRICK ON CATI

ALTHOUGH TWM never played a trick on Gwendolen again, he could sometimes play a few tricks on his mother!

One fine summer's day, when Twm was eight years old, Cati was sitting in her favourite place on the swing under the apple tree. Her new boyfriend, Jac lay on the grass by her side chewing a straw. Jumping down from the swing, Cati said in her happy-go-lucky way,

'Let's go down to the Old Bull Inn for a drink Jac.'

'Alright,' said Jac getting to his feet, 'I fancy a sit down by the side of the river, before going back to Jasper Tyler's farm.' Jac was a farmer's hand and it was the busy haymaking time.

'Can I come too, Mam?' asked Twm. He was sitting near the door, playing Jackstones and was listening to the conversation between Cati and Jac.

'No, you can't,' said Jac, 'you don't always have to be dragging behind your mother's skirts. Go and play with children your own age.' Twm looked hard at Jac, but said nothing. He didn't take kindly to Jac or to his relationship with his mother. Jac was always trying to get rid of Twm and Twm didn't like it.

Twm got up and strolled along the lane, picking a blackberry here and there and thinking hard about getting back at Jac. As he mused, he saw his friend Watt strolling towards him.

'Hello Twm,' said his friend, 'I'm on my way to see if Jasper Tyler wants any help with the haymaking. I could use some pocket money.'

'Make it another time and I'll come with you,' said Twm. 'But I need your help.' He drew his friend towards him and put his arm around his shoulder. The two continued down the lane towards the Old Bull Inn, Twm whispering in Watt's ear as they went. Watt started to giggle and then to chuckle and then laughed out loud.

'Hush,' said Twm, 'or the plan won't work.'

Cati and Jac sat on the bench in front of a great oak table drinking their beer.

'Look at them, making eyes at each other,' said

Twm crossly, 'I didn't think my mother could be so foolish.'

Twm and Watt moved across to a group of children playing Black-Jack. Soon Twm had explained his plan to them. Twm took a peeled thorn spike and hid it in his hand. He wandered back to the pub with Watt. Cati and Jac didn't even notice them, they were so close together looking into each other's eyes, whispering and giggling. Twm sneaked round behind his mother and her friend and quietly pinned their coat tails together with the thorn spike. Then he gave a signal to his friend Watt and the group of children outside the pub. They all began shouting,

'Mad bull! Mad bull!'

At the same time, they pushed into the pub a little trotting calf. The young calf reared and capered right up to the table where Cati and Jac sat. Cati screamed as she and Jac leapt to their feet. They fell over because they were pinned together by the thorn spike. Cati sat on the floor rubbing her leg. She soon realised that her son had played a joke on them and started laughing. But Jac was not so amused. When Cati had fallen to the floor, she had pulled Jac's coat from

him because they were joined together by the thorn spike. The truth is that Jac felt very self-conscious about the thin vest he was wearing underneath his coat, so he felt rather ridiculous.

'Oh, come on Jac,' said Cati, when she saw his scowling face, 'it's only a bit of fun and Twm is just a child.'

'It's a pity you don't control him better then,' said Jac as he stalked off in a very bad humour. Cati watched him departing, thinking that he was very poor at taking a joke. She was in truth not really keen on him and more in tune with her son's sense of fun. Twm watched to see how she would react. Affectionately, she put her arm round her son's shoulder.

'Come on Twm,' she said, 'plenty more fish in the sea. Come on everyone, let's go home and have some supper.'

So they all went back to Fountain Gate laughing and singing.

And Twm and Watt sang the loudest.

MAY DAY

TWM AND WATT strolled down the streets of Tregaron. Twm had now grown into a fine handsome young man. He and Watt were the best of friends. Watt liked Twm's company, he liked his friend's sharp wit and his sense of fun, and he knew that Twm would always help a friend in trouble.

'May Day tomorrow then,' said Watt.

'Yes,' sighed Twm, 'my mother is busy preparing for the Twmpath, and the dancing, but Jasper Tyler is too mean to give us a pig for the hog roast.'

'He doesn't like May Day,' said Watt, 'he's taken on the English ways.'

The two friends passed by Jasper Tyler's fields and vaulted over the stile. As they wandered through the fields, they heard Jasper's pigs grunting as they swilled round in their daily breakfast mush. They wandered along to watch the pigs feeding.

'They look pretty healthy,' said Twm. One pig looked at them sideways out of its little piggy eye and gave what sounded like a derisive snort. Then it went back to its noisy guzzling.

'That looks like a particularly healthy fat hog,' said Twm musingly. 'There's plenty of meat on him.' He looked at the large tusks and vicious teeth as the animal swilled around in the mush. The hog snorted and its head swung up and down as if it had heard Twm's words.

Twm took hold of Watt's arm and led him away from the pig's trough.

'I have an idea,' he said. He wandered down to the side of the stream and gathered up some fine loose sand which he put into his pocket. Then he and Watt strolled back up to the pigsty.

Twm stood by the gate and looked over at the pig. He brought some mushrooms out of his pocket and held them out invitingly. The pig turned its snout in the direction of Twm's hand and sniffed but pretended to take no notice. Twm began to make pig-like noises while still holding out his hand full of mushrooms towards the hog. Eventually the pig walked slowly towards Twm and the mushrooms. As it moved nearer,

Twm beckoned to Watt to scramble under the gate on the other side where he could get at the pig's tail, while Twm carefully climbed over the gate to get nearer to the beast. The pig moved nearer to Twm until he could smell its breath. When it was near enough for Twm to grab its ears, he gave Watt the signal and Watt grabbed the tail. The pig squealed loudly, but of course Twm knew that the farm hands were all out in the fields with no-one near enough to hear it. Only the servants up in the Big House were anywhere near enough to the pig sty and they were chattering and singing, making ready for the May Day celebrations in the Great Hall.

Twm's thick brown hair fell forward over his face as he and Watt wrestled silently with the pig. Although Twm was slightly built, he had a lithe strength and the friends managed to bring the animal to its knees. Twm carefully poured a little of the sand into its ears. The pig squealed again as it struggled to its feet. Then both friends opened the gate and began to make a great din to raise the alarm. Their shouts and hoorahs together with the squeals of the pig brought the farmer and his men rushing to the pigsty.

'What's the matter?' cried Jasper Tyler running down to the pigsty.

'Something is the matter with this pig,' gasped Twm, pretending to try to catch the animal to take it back to its sty. But the pig ran round and round in circles squealing. The farmer and his men all tried to catch the pig to no avail. The pig kept running round and round squealing and threatening the men with its huge teeth and tusks.

'I don't know what's the matter with the beast,' grunted the farmer.

'Do you think the devil has got into it?' Twm's dark brown eyes were anxious. 'You know the Bible story about the devil getting into a herd of swine. Jesus drove the evil spirit into them and they all rushed down to the cliffs and jumped into the sea. If you don't get rid of this one, he might pass the devil on to the others,' he added innocently.

'I think you are right,' said Jasper, impressed with Twm's knowledge of the Bible. 'This hog is behaving strangely, I've never seen him like this before. If we don't get rid of it, maybe the rest of the pigs will be affected in the same way. I don't want to take that risk, we must despatch it as soon as we can.'

'And bury it quickly,' added Twm, 'so that it is completely out of harm's way.'

Jasper Tyler instructed his men to help. The hog was strong and vicious and struggled hard, but they finally succeeded in bringing the beast to its knees and brought it down. One of them despatched it with a sharp knife, then they put it in a sack and buried it in a corner of the field. Twm and Watt helped.

'Come up to the house for a jug of ale,' said Jasper, 'you must be thirsty after all that work.' So the farmhands and the two friends followed Jasper to the kitchen and slaked their thirst with the sparkling honey gold beer.

'Thank you sir,' said Twm politely to Jasper, 'we'll be getting home now.'

'I hope you don't intend to take part in any of those pagan May Day celebrations tomorrow, Twm,' said Jasper Tyler. He came down hard on the villagers if he discovered them celebrating old customs. Bishop Rowland Lee, King Henry's man, had richly rewarded Jasper Tyler for his service to the crown of England, with position, money and land in Tregaron. Although Rowland Lee was now dead, others in England had taken his place.

'If I find any of that Welsh nonsense round here, I'll see to it that the culprits are caught and hanged,' said the Squire.

'No Sir,' said Twm stoutly, 'me and my Mam never have anything to do with that foolery.' Watt looked at Twm with surprise. He opened his mouth to say something, but Twm kicked him in the ankle.

The two friends took their leave and returned

to Fountain Gate where Cati and her mother were busy making cakes for the following day.

'Where have you been Twm?' she asked.

'Wandering about with Watt,' said Twm innocently. 'What are we having to eat at the Twmpath tomorrow?' he asked. The smell of the beautiful Welsh cakes on the griddle and the Bara Brith coming out of the oven was making his mouth water.

'Well, we have plenty of good bread, puddings, ale and cakes as you can see, but I'm afraid we will not have any hog roast this year. Jasper Tyler won't let us have one of his pigs, since he's hand in glove with the English. He may punish us for taking part, if he can catch us, on the other hand he sometimes pretends to take no notice. It all depends on his mood I suppose. You can't trust him an inch. Anyway, we'll have to do without the meat this time I'm afraid.'

'I don't know about that,' said Twm with a smile, 'you never know what might turn up.'

That night when it was almost pitch black, some figures could be seen moving stealthily down to the corner of the farmer's field. It was Twm, Watt, Owen and Rhys.

'Come on boys,' said Twm as they reached the place where the pig was buried. 'It's not that far down under the ground.' The friends worked silently digging up the earth until they got to the dead pig. They tugged and pulled until they had dragged the animal free of the earth, then they tied some rope around it and began to pull it away towards the village.

Jasper Tyler stirred uneasily in his bed. In his nightmare, he watched his pigs as they rushed down to the cliffs and flung themselves into the sea.

Next day dawned bright and clear. The sky was a clear pale blue, the air still. As Cati looked out of the window she saw a single blackthorn leaf sway slightly in the early summer breeze.

'It's going to be another hot day,' said her mother, she was looking quite frail thought Cati. 'I don't like this weather, it takes away all my energy.'

'It doesn't seem to affect Twm,' smiled Cati. Twm was swinging from the old apple tree with Watt by his side.

'Right, let's get going,' said Cati. 'We have to

put all these things into the dog cart and get them to the village green.' The things referred to were bunting for the May Pole, ropes for the tug-of-war and Cati's harp.

'Come on Twm,' cried his mother, 'we'll be late.' Twm and Watt ran indoors.

'I'll carry the harp,' said Twm.

'Be careful then,' said his mother, 'we only have the one and I don't want it broken.'

'I'll help with the bunting,' said Watt and busily began to roll the multi-coloured material down through the kitchen and out of the door towards the waiting cart. Cati's pony, Cothi, stood patiently while the cart was loaded up ready for the festivities. The family piled into the back of the cart and Cothi began trotting along the street towards the village green, the Twmpath Chwarae.

'Come on,' said Cati, 'let's have a song.'

As they neared the village green, Cati began to sniff the air.

'What's that wonderful smell?' she said. The smell of roasting meat was wafting through the air.

'It smells like roast pig,' Twm said innocently.

'You're right,' said Cati wonderingly, then she saw her son's engaging smile.

'What have you been up to?' she said as they arrived at the field and saw the dancing flames of the fire and the hog turning on the spit.

'Me, Mam?' said Twm innocently. 'I haven't done a thing.' Cati laughed. 'I know you can charm the birds off the trees Twm Siôn, but you can't fool me,' she said. 'Still, it's a wonderful thing to have a hog roast on May Day. It puts the cap on all our fun and games.'

And they had the best day they had had for many a long year.

ELIAS

TWM ENJOYED his young days in Fountain Gate. His mother, Cati, was a pretty girl who loved having fun. She enjoyed the company of young boys like Jac, but the real love of her life was her son Twm.

Cati's house rang with the sound of laughter and music. The door was always open to friends, neighbours and visitors, and Cati generously shared her meals with them. They enjoyed whatever she happened to have in the house; it might be a feast or it might be next to nothing, depending on her changing fortune. Cati didn't mind being poor but she liked to be independent. She received some money from her work as a schoolteacher, but if the parents sometimes had no money to pay her for their children's schooling, she often accepted payment in kind, and they gave her whatever they could afford, such as meat or fruit or clothes.

Twm loved his life in Tregaron and inherited his mother's sense of fun, although he sometimes wondered about his father. Cati never spoke of him.

Twm roamed free around the countryside and the hills outside the town of Tregaron. Sometimes he took his friend Watt with him for company, but most of the time, he and his pony Cothi went riding alone.

One day he was riding along a hillside south of Tregaron at a place called Dinas. He had reached the River Tywi and dismounted. He tied Cothi loosely to a tree and sat on the river bank listening to the birdsong. He watched the clear water cascading over the rocks as he listened to its pleasant rushing sound. Lazily he spotted a dipper as it pecked its way along the bottom of the river looking for food. The sun shone, the air was clear and fresh, Twm lay back on the grass and thought himself the luckiest person in the world to live in this beautiful place.

He stood up and stretched himself before picking up the reins and leaping on Cothi's back. He turned the pony's head towards the summit of the hills, meaning to explore as high as Cothi could climb. The pony scrambled gamely along the slopes and the scree, as Twm looked up and spotted some large rocks stretching upwards to the sky. He urged Cothi onwards and horse and rider climbed higher and higher until the horse could go no further. Twm dismounted, and scrambled a little higher leaving Cothi standing patiently waiting below. Twm stopped in front of two large rocks like pillars with a crevice between. Curiously he clambered and pushed himself through the aperture and found himself inside a large, cosy cave!

'This is splendid,' he said to himself. 'I could hide here for ever and no-one would find me!'

He looked up and saw the sky above him, then he lay back and watched the blue sky and white clouds until he began to doze. Cothi contentedly cropped the short grass below the cave as Twm lay on the ground drowsing in his new found home. It was a warm summer's day. He wondered how his friend Watt was getting on. He hadn't seen him for some time. Reluctantly, he decided that it was time to return to Tregaron, so he got up, shook the dust from his clothes and climbed out of the cave.

He mounted Cothi once more and turned towards the path leading down the hillside towards the track leading to Tregaron. As he rode, he began to think of some of the tricks he had played on people from the time he was very small, like the time he had jumped out from behind the pigsty and frightened Gwenni with the skull mask or the time he and Watt had played the trick on his mother and Jac in the Old Bull Inn.

When he got home, he led Cothi to his stable at the back of the house, rubbed him down and gave him food and water. The he went into the house and dragged out the big box from the corner of his bedroom. It was full of clothes and masks and different kinds of hats, and Twm began rummaging inside. He thought he might go down to the village to see how things were without being recognised himself!

Later that day, a beggar limped into the village, and stopped beside the inn, watching the villagers coming and going. No-one took any notice of the poor old man leaning against the door whittling away at some wood in his hand.

He looked across at Elias Richards' shop. Elias sold all kinds of wares, food, clothes, china, pots and pans. Elias was the meanest man in Tregaron. Suddenly the beggarly old man heard a commotion from inside the shop and Elias emerged clutching a youth by his breeches. The shopkeeper flung the boy out onto the pavement where he lay on the ground rubbing his backside.

'Be off with you,' shouted Elias, 'you're lucky I am not carting you off to the Squire's jail, you thieving ruffian.' Twm looked at the youth's grimy face.

'Watt,' he said, clearing his throat, 'over here.' Watt looked round him, he thought he heard the voice of his friend Twm. He looked up and down the street but all he could see was the old man leaning against the corner of the street whittling away at his piece of wood.

'Over here,' said Twm again. Watt stared at the old man in disbelief.

'Be careful,' said Twm warningly, 'enemy about.' He watched Elias strolling across the pavement from his shop towards the tavern.

'Make your way down to the fields at the back of Fountain Gate,' he said.

Watt stumbled to his feet without looking again at Twm and made his way along the road

towards Fountain Gate. Shortly afterwards Twm began to limp slowly in the opposite direction. But as soon as he was out of sight of spying eyes, Twm retraced his steps and quickly joined Watt.

'Well, what were you up to back there in the old skinflint's shop? How are things with you?' he said affectionately.

'As bad as they can be,' sighed Watt. 'Since the business with the May Day Twmpath, Jasper Tyler has been even more ruthless with all of us in the village. He won't give me any work on his farm, and he and Elias are making our lives as miserable as they can, making sure that we have no money or food. We are starving most of the time. Elias flung me out of his shop as soon as he saw me looking at some of the food on his shelf. Actually, I had my eye on a beautiful looking pitcher in the corner of the shop. If I could get hold of that, then I could get a lot of money for it on market day.'

'I think we can come up with a plan between us,' said Twm with a smile. 'Let's put our heads together. It will be like old times. Let's go back to Fountain Gate and see what other disguise we can find, and then we'll tackle Master Elias!'

A little over an hour later, two travellers could be seen riding up the main street. They looked well dressed with stout leather boots, black doublet and breeches, and a smart cap with a large feather at the side. They rode up to the tethering post opposite Elias's shop and dismounted. They carefully tethered the horses before strolling nonchalantly across to Elias's shop, and glancing in through the window. The two young men wandered inside, and began examining the wares displayed along the shelves. They moved towards the corner where the shopkeeper kept the pitchers. Twm picked up one of the pitchers and examined it closely.

'A good buy there sir,' said Elias, coming forward and eager to make a sale. Twm said nothing and continued to examine the vessel. He held it up high and looked down inside it.

'I can see a hole in it, shop keeper,' he said sternly. 'Would you sell me a dud pot?' He continued to examine another of the pots standing on the shelf, leaving the shopkeeper to look for the hole in the first pot. But, out of the corner of his eye, Twm watched Watt quietly pick up another pitcher and make his way towards the door. Twm moved around so that he manoeuvred Elias into a position where he had his back to the door while he continued to examine the pitcher that Twm had complained about.

'I can see nothing wrong with it,' he said mystified.

'Put your hand down inside and you can feel the hole,' said Twm.

Elias put his hand deep inside the pitcher.

'I still can't feel anything,' he said exasperated. By this time Twm and Watt had moved nearer to the door.

'If there is no hole,' said Twm with a twinkle in his eye, 'how can you get your hand inside?'

With that, Twm laughing, left the shop, marched briskly across the road, leapt onto his horse's back and rode away. Elias followed him to the door, where he was pushed aside by Watt, who followed Twm, the two of them riding along the main street. Elias returned to his shop and looked around at his goods. He saw that the pitchers appeared to have been disturbed. He began to count them and grew angrier as he realised that the 'travellers' had duped him and stolen one of his pitchers. But he hadn't recognised either Twm or Watt in their excellent disguises.

'He wouldn't miss it,' thought Twm as he rode away, 'and Watt would paint it another colour and sell it at the next market. It would bring in a lot of money for Watt and his family to buy food and clothes.'

Twm did not go back to Tregaron. He and Watt separated and Twm made for his cave, concealed deep in the Dinas hillside. Better to keep a low profile he thought until the heat died down.

Elias and his men searched for the robbers high and low. If they had found the thieves, they would have been imprisoned or even put to death, but of course Twm had been too clever for them, and they failed. In spite of Elias's fury they were forced to give up the search and return home empty handed.

'I will catch those thieves one day,' Elias vowed, 'and I will see them hang.'

THE MARI LWYD

I T WAS A VERY cold Twelfth Night. Snow lay thick on the ground outside Fountain Gate. Twm gazed through the window as Cati and her friends prepared the Mari Lwyd.

'We'll have to be extra careful this evening,' said Jac, 'Jasper Tyler turned a blind eye to our May Day Twmpath and the hog roast, although he may have suspected something about the pig. I think Twm had a hand in that, but I don't know how he did it.'

Jac looked across at Twm who was sitting on the floor near Cati's dressing-up box. He was pulling out masks and trying them on. He looked across at Watt who continued practising on his fiddle. Twm said seriously, 'Jasper didn't say anything because he is superstitious and he thought the pig he killed would bring bad luck. Even if he suspected that we had dug it up, and used it for the hog roast, he wouldn't say anything because he probably hoped that it would bring us bad luck.' Twm chuckled, 'It wasn't the devil in the pig,' he said, 'it was a few grains of sand in its ear.'

'You need to be careful,' said Jac, 'he will catch you one day and then you will be for the high jump.' He crossed his hand across his throat.

'Don't do that!' cried Cati, 'not even in jest.'

'Jac's right,' said Eifion, one of his friends. 'You know what they are, Rowland Lee may be dead, but the English are just as bad without him. They are determined to stop us doing anything in the old Welsh ways and Jasper is hand in glove with them, he wants to protect his ill-gotten gains. They want us all to turn English.'

'That will take some doing,' said Elizabeth as she started tying ribbons on the Mari.

'Maybe the cold weather will keep them away,' said Cati. She was quietly strumming her harp.

Jac was busy working on the Mari Lwyd. This was a horse's skull which Eifion and Jac had buried in quick lime twelve months previously. When they had pulled it out earlier that morning, the skull had turned dead white. The two men brought it round to Cati's house and now they were dressing the Mari Lwyd to lead her round to each of the houses in Tregaron.

'How's that?' said Jac as he fixed the lower jaw with a spring which made the mouth open and shut with a loud snap.

'Very frightening,' laughed Eifion. He stuck a pole about five foot long into the bottom of the horse's skull and Twm draped a white sheet over it. Elizabeth and Cati decorated it with coloured ribbons.

'I found these pieces of glass down by the stream,' said Elizabeth, 'they will make fine eyes,' and she placed them on either side of the horse's head.

'And these will do for two black ears,' said Cati. She pinned two pieces of cloth underneath the glass eyes.

'Well, the Mari is ready,' said Twm. 'Come on Eifion.'

Eifion stood underneath the sheet holding the pole; he operated the lower jaw of the skull from inside the sheet to make the mouth open and shut.

'How does she look?' he said, his voice sounded muffled coming from underneath the white sheet.

'Very good,' said Cati admiringly. She placed the reins over the Mari's head.

'Here you are Jac,' she said, 'you take them. You can lead the party tonight.'

'Thanks Cati,' said Jac, 'I'm looking forward to this evening, we'll all have a good time calling on our neighbours. We'll have some good songs and some good beer.'

'As long as the English don't catch us,' said Elizabeth.

'We can always pull the wool over the eyes of the English,' said Eifion, 'but Jasper Tyler and Elias Richards are spies and traitors,' he spat contemptuously. 'They know about our ways and where we go, it's more difficult to give them the slip.'

'Elias Richards is getting worse than Jasper Tyler,' said Elizabeth. 'Especially since that business with the stolen pitcher, he never did find the thieves.' She looked at Twm, but he was busy trying on a hawk mask. She continued, 'Only yesterday, he gave Lloyd some sugar as payment for cleaning his shop, but the sugar was full of ants, and Lloyd and his grandfather, Old Dilwyn had to throw it away.'

'He would cheat his own mother,' said Cati contemptuously, 'but he does have strong servants to protect him and Jasper does encourage him to arrest people for thieving.' Twm said nothing, he appeared to be concentrating on putting some finishing touches to a face mask.

'We could be arrested this evening,' said Elizabeth seriously.

'We'll think of something,' said Cati, 'we always do, and no English spies or Welsh traitors are going to stop us from keeping up the old ways.' Her face was determined.

'That's right Mam,' said Twm, 'we'll show them.' Twm was usually sunny tempered, with a good natured smile, but at this moment his face was serious.

'Yes,' said Eifion, 'we'll show them a thing or two.' He paused, 'Right, are we ready?'

The party trooped out of Fountain Gate and gathered outside in the cold night air. Eifion stood underneath the white draped sheet, holding the pole. Jac held the reins. Cati, Elizabeth, Twm and Watt stood behind. Watt carried his fiddle and Cati held her harp in her hand. Twm and Watt wore masks.

They walked from Fountain Gate down the street towards Hywel Dafydd's house with Jac leading the Mari and the others singing and playing their instruments. They were a fine sight with Watt playing his fiddle in time to the Mari's steps. The night was frosty and most people were in their warm houses enjoying the festive season in their own way.

The Mari Lwyd stopped outside Hywel's house, and Cati and Watt stopped playing; they all listened quietly. They could hear their neighbours laughing and singing inside.

'They are having a good time,' whispered Watt.

Jac knocked loudly on the door with the stick he carried in his hand. He called out the special greeting asking Hywel to allow the Mari Lwyd into his house so that they could join in the fun and share their food and drink.

At first, Hywel pretended that he did not know who they were and refused to let in 'strangers'.

'Come on,' coaxed Jac, 'you know that you must let us in or the Mari will bring bad luck.'

The door opened and Hywel stood there smiling. 'Come on in, Mari Lwyd,' he said, 'you are always welcome in my house.'

Jac led the Mari inside and the rest followed.

'Give us a song then,' said Hywel. And the Mari Lwyd party sang and played the old Welsh songs with all their heart. Then Hywel invited them to sit down and share their festive food and drink. They sat on wooden benches and passed round a beautiful wassail bowl which was brought out for special occasions. It was full to the brim. Pieces of fruit floated in the honeyed gold ale.

Happily, they passed the time in this way with Hywel and his family for half an hour before they decided it was time to move on to the next house in the street. As they left Hywel, they gave the Mari Lwyd farewell:

'A Happy New Year to you all. We wish you joy, may you prosper every day in every way.'

No-one noticed grey shadows flitting along

behind them. Jasper Tyler's men had followed them stealthily and were lying in wait.

'The Mari Lwyd won't bring good luck this time,' whispered Trefor Richards the leader of the gang. 'Get them boys, and we'll have a rich reward from the Squire for this night's work.' Trefor was Elias's son and had a few scores to settle with the villagers of Tregaron.

There were twenty of Jasper's men and Eifion and Jac didn't stand a chance. The men knocked them unconscious. Cati and Elizabeth fled in panic. Twm and Watt melted into the darkness of the night. The men kicked and trampled the Mari Lwyd until it was nothing but a heap of wood and bones. The ribbons were buried deep in the snow. They stamped on Cati's harp breaking it to pieces. They dragged Eifion's and Jac's senseless bodies to a waiting cart.

There was a terrible knocking at Hywel's door. The door remained firmly shut, the house was silent, but it was to no avail. The men kicked down the door and pushed their way inside. They dragged out Hywel and his two sons, William and Hugh.

'It's prison for you ruffians,' said Trefor, 'or worse. It depends on how the hangman feels when he gets here in the morning, but I don't hold out much hope.' His voice was heavy with sarcasm and he made a gesture across his throat with his hand.

'As much as I hate the English,' said Hywel grimly, 'I have nothing but contempt for you. You are Welsh and ought to be ashamed of yourselves.'

He said no more as Trefor hit him on the head with his large heavy stick and Hywel dropped unconscious on to the cold snow. William rushed to his side but he was pulled away by two men as Trefor dragged his father to the waiting cart. Trefor and his ruffians hauled Hywel, William and Hugh up and threw them on top of Eifion and Jac, who lay still and senseless in the back of the cart. Trefor jumped up in front and slapped the reins of the black Welsh pony.

'Come on you beauty,' he said, 'off we go, we've done a good night's work here and should be paid handsomely for this job.'

Meirion jumped up beside him. 'We haven't found Twm Siôn Cati yet,' he said.

'Let's get these fools tied up in prison first,' said Trefor, 'We'll soon find the other ruffians.' His voice was confident and cocky. Meirion was silent. 'He's given the slip to better men than you,' he thought, but he knew it was best to keep his own counsel with a man like Trefor Richards.

The singing had stopped in all the houses as the horse and cart rumbled down the icy cold streets of Tregaron towards the jail house.

THE BULL IN THE BARN

THE SQUIRE'S MEN searched in vain but Twm and Watt had vanished. If they had looked in the right places they might have seen two figures on horseback riding up the scree and shale on the slopes of Dinas.

'Where are we going?' panted Watt.

'Somewhere we cannot be found,' replied Twm grimly.

It was a steep and hazardous climb but eventually the two friends reached the place below the cave. Twm and Watt dismounted and Twm led his friend further up the hillside towards the cave.

'Come on,' Twm cried, 'we're nearly there.' He pulled Watt through the crevice. They slipped and slid, grabbing onto pieces of rock and tufty growths of plants to avoid falling backwards. Finally they reached the floor of the cave and threw themselves down on the ground, out of breath.

Watt looked around him. The walls of the cave rose above him some twenty feet. As he looked upward he could see the sky.

'Well, Watt,' said Twm grinning, 'Jasper Tyler won't find us here!'

'How on earth did you find this place?' asked Watt amazed.

'To tell the truth,' said Twm, 'I stumbled across it by accident, while I was out one day riding Cothi.'

'Well,' said Watt, laughing, 'I doubt whether anyone will ever find you here.' The two friends sat on the ground with their backs against the wall of the cave.

'What do you think has happened to Eifion and Jac?' asked Watt. 'I imagine that Trefor Richards has carted them off to jail,' said Twm grimly.

'No doubt expecting a rich reward from Jasper Tyler,' said Watt.

'Trefor needs to be taught a lesson,' said Twm musingly, 'and his employer.' We must think of something special this time, to hit the Squire's pocket and punish Trefor and his gang. Doesn't Jasper have a prize bull?'

'Yes,' said Watt, 'but he keeps it under close guard. He expects to take it to market soon and get a lot of money for it. I don't see how we could get anywhere near it, let alone steal it!'

Twm lay back against the rock and closed his eyes. Watt thought he had gone to sleep! After a while Twm began to chuckle, he sat up and said, 'I think I have a plan to settle with Trefor and Jasper Tyler, listen to this . . .' He and Watt began talking and planning together while Twm drew sketches on the dry dust of the floor of the cave.

As dusk fell on Dinas, two shadowy figures rode silently down the rocky slopes and through the trees until they reached the marshland. It was Twm and Watt. They made their way quietly along the roadside towards Jasper Tyler's farm, keeping to the hedges and ditches so that they would not be seen by prying eyes. Finally they reached the Squire's big barn. Dismounting, Twm and Watt crept the last few yards and lay full length on the ground looking for signs of life. They could hear the sound of Jasper's prize bull snorting and shuffling round inside.

'He sounds like a fine beast,' whispered Watt.

'He is,' said Twm, 'he comes from Jasper's best stock, specially nurtured.' He laid his finger on his lips, 'Look out,' he whispered, 'I can see the guards. It looks as if Jasper has picked his best men, Trefor and Meirion. This works out better than I hoped. They will get the blame for losing the bull. Won't Jasper be mad!' Twm started to chuckle again. He watched as the two men strode up and down in front of the barn door, one carried a pike, the other a strong stout staff.

Twm and Watt shuffled along on their bellies until they were at the back of the barn out of sight of the Squire's men. Suddenly, Twm and Watt stood up.

'Fire! Fire!' they shouted.

Trefor and Meirion stood stock still. They

looked at the barn. They could see no sign of smoke rising.

'Come on you witless sluggards,' the voice came from the direction of the Big House, it sounded like Jasper Tyler.

'Do you want me to lose my prize bull because of your dawdling?' Twm had mimicked Jasper's voice to perfection.

Galvanized into action, Trefor and Meirion charged through the barn door, and rushed for the buckets of water hanging on the side of the walls in case of fire. As soon as the door was open Watt and Twm slid inside jumped on the bull's back and drove him out of the barn.

Beside themselves with rage, Trefor and Meirion ran after them, but in vain. They rushed to the big bell hanging in the yard and pulled it for all they were worth, raising the alarm. Men ran out of the smaller barns where they slept, hastily pulling on their trousers and shirts, making for their horses to pursue the thieves.

But Twm had created the panic he had planned and the men were in such disarray, that he and Watt were able to jump on to the bull's back and speed away to the woods before their pursuers could catch up with them.

He and Watt drove the bull into the thickest part of the trees and slid off its back. The bull was not best pleased with the treatment it had been having and pawed the ground, snorting dangerously and eyeing its tormentors. But Twm had handled such beasts many times and he had never let go of the large ring in its nose from the moment he had leapt on to its back. He continued to keep a tight hold on the heavy ring and the bull was forced to follow Twm wherever he led it. He tied the beast tightly to the stout trunk of a large oak tree.

'Now what do we do,' panted Watt. 'They will

soon find us, once they have located the tracks of the bull.'

'Take off your boots,' ordered Twm. Mystified, Watt obeyed. Twm did the same. Then he tied the boots on each of the bull's hooves back to front.

'Come on,' he said to his friend, 'up you go,' and he and Watt jumped on to the bull's back once more. They rode out and along the road towards Fountain Gate. But of course, because the boots were back to front, it looked as if the bull was going in the opposite direction! Dawn was breaking as Twm and Watt rode the bull past Fountain Gate to a suitable hiding place.

Old Dilwyn was one of the oldest residents in Tregaron and was always an early riser. He was walking along the street towards Elias's grocery store when he saw the two friends riding the bull through the village. He raised his hat to them as they sped by. He chuckled quietly to himself as he recognised Twm and Jasper's prize bull!

No sooner had the dust from the bull's hooves settled in the street than Jasper Tyler rode up with Trefor and Meirion. He pulled his horse up sharply in front of Old Dilwyn.

'Have you seen that impudent thief Twm Siôn Cati,' snapped Jasper Tyler. 'He will be hanged for sure when I catch him. He has stolen my prize bull.' Old Dilwyn was unsympathetic His sons had been caught long ago and punished by Jasper Tyler. They had been accused of stealing sheep, although Dilwyn had farmed the land for many years until it had been taken away from him by the English and given as a gift to Jasper Tyler. Old Dilwyn had a few scores of his own to settle with the Squire.

'I've seen no-one pass through here,' he replied, 'but I did hear how you broke up the Mari Lwyd party the other night. And our friends from the village have been taken away. That was a foolish thing to do Squire,' he added sagely, shaking his head. 'It does folk no good being unkind to the Mari Lwyd.' Old Dilwyn was so old that he knew that Jasper would let him get away with this kind of talk.

'Superstitious nonsense,' blustered the Squire, 'I am expected to keep the peace in this god-forsaken town and Twm Siôn Cati has overstepped the mark. I swear that this time, he will be brought to justice.'

He and his men turned their horses in the direction of the hills, they moved slowly following the bull's tracks, but of course because Twm had put the shoes on back to front, the tracks appeared to be going in the opposite direction to Fountain Gate! As they rode, the Squire seemed subdued by Old Dilwyn's words, he felt uncomfortable about flouting the Mari Lwyd.

It brought bad luck.

ELIAS AGAIN

'WHAT WILL YOU do with the bull?' asked Watt. He and Twm lay on the ground beneath the cave.

'I expect I will drive it to market when I am ready, suitably disguised of course!' he laughed. 'It's a small recompense for all the harm Jasper Tyler does to the folks around Dinas.'

'I don't know who is worst,' said Watt, 'Jasper Tyler or Elias Richards.'

'Not much to choose between them I suppose,' said Twm.

'I think Elias must be the meanest man in Tregaron,' persisted Watt. 'He gets people to work for him, then he pretends he has no money and gives them shop goods instead. Even then the goods are worthless. We lived well after I sold the pitcher we stole between us Twm, but when the money was gone and I could still not find any work, my sister offered to work for Elias, cleaning the shop. Last week, he gave her some flour and butter pretending he couldn't find any money for her, but when she got home there were weevils in the flour and the butter was rancid. The worst of all is that we can't do much about it.'

'Oh, I don't know,' said Twm thoughtfully.

A week or two after this conversation, Twm lounged against the corner of a shop in the main street of Tregaron. No-one would have recognised him, for he had disguised himself as a beggar. As he whittled away at a wooden pipe, he noticed Elias leading a fine stallion along the cobbled streets.

Twm looked thoughtfully at Elias as the man swaggered towards the inn. Elias was a small man with greasy black hair and shifty eyes. As he began to tie up his horse at the tethering post outside the inn, a ragged boy stepped in front of him, begging for money to buy a loaf of bread, but Elias flung him aside, striking him with his crop. Twm recognised the little beggar boy, his name was Lloyd and he was the grandson of Old Dilwyn. Twm watched the shop keeper disappear inside the inn, then looked thoughtfully at the fine grey stallion as the horse swished its tail and pawed the ground.

Twm looked casually about him. It was a warm
sunny day and most people were inside the inn
drinking ale and keeping cool. Quickly, he caught
up the reins of the grey stallion, leapt in the
saddle and galloped through the town towards
the hills above Tregaron.

A few hours later Elias emerged from the inn,
wiping away the last few drops of ale from his
whiskers. He staggered towards the place where
he had tethered his horse and stood in front of
the pole scratching his chin with amazement
when he saw that it was empty. He was quite
drunk and unsteady on his feet and he looked up
and down the street thinking the horse may
somehow have loosened its reins and might be
cropping the grass by the side of the road. But
stare as long as he might his horse was nowhere
to be seen. His face grew bright red and he began
to stamp up and down with rage.

'Someone has stolen my horse!' he screamed.
'When I find him he will pay with his life. We
know how to deal with horse thieves around
here.'

People gathered in the street to see what
the commotion was about, but Elias had little

sympathy from the local people. They listened to his tirade silently, glad in their hearts that someone had given him grief and hoping that he would never find his horse. With a bit of luck, he would have a long walk home!

As Elias was beginning to think that he would indeed have to start walking, he spied a man riding into town on a horse with a short cropped mane, its flanks and forelegs speckled black. The man dismounted and doffed his cap respectfully to Elias.

Elias looked at the poorly clothed man standing awkwardly in front of him. He was wearing a large broad brimmed hat which covered most of his face. The stranger turned and limped towards the inn, where he clumsily tied his piebald horse to the tethering post. An idea came into Elias's mind. If he could trick this simple looking soul into parting with his horse, he could ride home in comfort! The shop keeper pretended to appear interested in the stranger.

'Who might you be, good sir?' he asked politely, eyeing the horse at the same time.

'My name is Siôn, thank you for asking sir,' replied the stranger; he kept his face hidden but

Elias noticed an ugly scar running down the side of his face. No wonder he didn't want people to see him, he thought! 'I have a small farm two miles from here' continued Siôn. He began to move towards the inn as if he were about to seek some ale.

Elias stopped him, 'Did you see a rider and a fine grey stallion as you came into town? A thieving scoundrel stole it from under my nose.' He thought this made him look foolish. 'Actually,' he said, 'he stole him while I was inside the inn taking some refreshment.' Siôn looked sympathetic. 'That was a poor thing to do,' he said sympathetically, 'but I'm sorry to have to tell you that I've seen no-one on the road at all. I doubt whether you will ever see your horse again, these horse thieves are very clever at hiding their ill-gotten gains. I wish I could help you more,' he added, slapping his piebald on the rump, affectionately.

Elias eyed the horse longingly. Siôn continued, 'I shouldn't be sorry if some thief stole this miserable beast. He has a stubborn streak and travels no faster than a cart-horse. I'd gladly sell him for five sovereigns.' Elias studied the stallion's sturdy limbs and fine coat thinking that the horse looked quite strong and fit. He thought of the long journey ahead of him.

'Well it's as you say,' he said cunningly, 'your horse looks as if he might be troublesome especially if he is as stubborn as you say, but I need a beast to take me home. I'll probably have to sell him for slaughter afterwards, so I'll be generous and offer you two sovereigns.' Elias thought he could easily take advantage of such a simple sounding man. Siôn rubbed his chin thoughtfully.

'Well,' he said, 'you seem a good kind of person, and you are in some trouble without your own horse.' He hesitated for a moment, 'Alright', he said decisively 'it's a bargain.'

They shook hands. Elias handed over the two sovereigns and took the reins of his new horse. He leapt into the saddle and rode away over the hills homeward bound.

As soon as he disappeared, Siôn took off his broad brimmed hat and rumpled coat, wiping away the scar from the side of his face he looked across at Watt. Watt had been leaning against the wall beside the inn watching Elias striking his bargain with Siôn.

Watt started to laugh and slap his sides in glee, and soon all the other people watching did the same, for Siôn, as you may have guessed, was none other than Twm Siôn Cati in disguise!

Twm strolled towards the inn with his friend, tossing one of the two sovereigns to the little beggar boy who had been so badly treated by the rich merchant.

'Here you are, Lloyd,' Twm cried, 'here is one of his own sovereigns, a bit more than you asked for and Elias none the wiser.'

'Thanks Twm,' cried the boy, 'I'll be able to buy plenty of food with this, for me and Grandad. Why don't you come to our house tonight and share a meal with us?'

'Thanks all the same,' laughed Twm, 'but I have a bit more work to do this evening.'

Twm strolled inside the tavern and threw the other gold sovereign on the counter. 'Drinks for everybody!' he cried. 'I don't think Elias, the old goat, will be too pleased when the paint starts to fade on that 'piebald' I sold him! When that happens he'll find the horse he bought from me is none other than his own grey stallion!'

The villagers in Tregaron roared with laughter at the way Twm had tricked the miserly shopkeeper and they spent the rest of the evening pleasantly, telling jokes and singing old Welsh songs.

*

When Elias walked round to his stable the following day, he couldn't believe his eyes. Standing quietly in the stall was his own stallion, and the piebald he had bought from Twm was nowhere to be seen! Then he spied the reins dangling from the horse's neck. They were the same as the ones he had held when he rode the piebald home the previous evening! He realised that he had been tricked and his face turned purple with rage.

'I know the scoundrel who played this trick on me!' he fumed. 'It was that good-for-nothing Twm Siôn Cati. Everyone in the village knows how much he likes to play tricks on people. He even made his mother look foolish once, when she was with her boyfriend in the Old Bull Inn.' His son, Trefor, was watching his father pacing up and down. He knew he had a wicked temper and he didn't want to cross him and make him worse. Trefor and Twm were much the same age and had disliked each other from their school days.

'What can you do father,' he tried to speak soothingly, he was afraid of his father's evil temper, Elias could easily turn on him or his mother.

'Do?' he shouted. 'Do? I am going down to

his house, Fountain Gate, at Tregaron. We'll see if he will have the courage to brave me face to face instead of trying his sly tricks!' Still quivering with rage, Elias stormed out of the house, leapt on his horse once more and galloped off to Tregaron.

As he approached Fountain Gate, an old man shuffled by as Elias reined in his horse. 'I'm looking for Twm Siôn Cati,' Elias said with a scowl.

The old man chuckled, 'Well,' he whispered, 'this is his house,' his voice sounded hoarse. 'But, knowing his sly ways, I expect that when you knock on the front door, he will make his escape around the back.' The angry shop keeper thought that the old man was probably right and decided to thwart that plan by striding round to the back of the house, expecting to catch Twm as he tried to run away.

As soon as Elias disappeared round to the back of the house, the old man threw off the ragged clothes he was wearing and there again was Twm, laughing fit to burst! He leaped on Elias's horse and galloped across the fields to the shop keeper's own house. Dismounting, he hammered urgently on the door. Elias's wife, Enid answered the door and looked at Twm in some amazement.

'Pardon me Ma'am,' said Twm politely, 'your husband has sent me on an urgent errand from the market in Tregaron. He is bidding for a new prize bull and needs thirty sovereigns from his coffers.' Enid looked dubiously at Twm. 'Look, he said, 'he has given me his silver-handled whip and his fine horse so that you can see that I am trusted by him.'

Twm smiled at Enid pleasantly. She looked at the silver-handled whip, the horse and again at Twm. He looked innocently at her with his frank blue eyes. She didn't hesitate any more but disappeared into the house returning with the golden coins. Placing them carefully in a leather purse tied to his belt, Twm thanked her and galloped away.

Unfortunately for Twm, Enid was not quite happy about the stranger and his persuasive manner. She called to Elias's men to follow Twm to make sure that he delivered the money as he had said. They tracked Twm out of town as he galloped along the dusty track leading to the distant hills.

They were too many for Twm and he was quickly surrounded. The men pulled him off his horse and dragged him back to Elias who delightedly threw him into jail.

'Got you at last,' gloated Elias. 'I have a good many scores to settle with you Twm Siôn Cati, and Jasper will be delighted to see you in jail. You'll hang tomorrow for sure as soon as the hangman arrives from Aberystwyth.'

TWM IN JAIL

TWM KNEW THAT he was in deep trouble as he lay on the ground in the jail, rubbing his shoulder with a grimace.

He looked around him. The cell was pitch black, there were no windows and the walls smelled musty and damp. He heard a scuffling sound and two small bright eyes stared at him from the darkness. As his eyes grew accustomed to the gloom, he made out the figure of a long brown rat!

After a while he lost track of the time, and began to doze. In his half sleep, he thought he heard a tapping on the wall behind him. He pressed his ear against the cold stone and listened.

'Is that you Twm?' he recognised Eifion's voice.

'Yes,' replied Twm, 'are you on your own?'

'No,' replied Eifion, 'Jac is here with me, and Hywel and his two boys. Have they caught you at last Twm?' he continued, 'if so, we are all done for.' His voice sounded desperate.

'It takes more than Jasper's jail to finish me off,' said Twm, feeling braver than he felt. 'Don't lose heart my friend.' He stopped, he heard footsteps outside his cell. 'Hush,' he said, 'someone's coming.' He heard the great keys turning in the lock and the jailer appeared. The jailer was a man from Caio called Elphin. Behind him, in the gloom, Twm saw a dark figure hidden in a long black cloak.

'You have a visitor,' said the jailer.

Twm sat up rubbing his eyes. The stranger stepped into the cell. A large black hat and scarf hid his face, only his eyes were visible. Twm would have recognised those eyes anywhere, they belonged to Jasper Tyler.

'That will be all my good man,' said the stranger in a low hoarse voice, he gave Elphin a silver coin. 'We don't want to be disturbed.'

'Very good sir,' Elphin replied obediently and immediately left the two men, rubbing his silver coin gleefully.

Jasper Tyler looked around him with distaste.

'How do you like your new home?' he asked Twm.

'A little more comfortable than yours, I think, but while people like you are in power, this is the home of true Welshmen,' replied Twm nonchalantly. 'I'd offer you a seat and some wine but, as you can see, I am a little out of funds at the moment.'

'You may speak rashly,' responded Jasper 'but you do know that you are to hang tomorrow. I am the only man who can save you, and I'm unlikely to lift a finger to help you. You and your friends repeatedly steal from me and Elias Richards and we are trying to uphold the law.'

'You know why we are forced to do such things,' said Twm, 'you do not keep the laws of the people of Wales and you starve us and take our land away. But you are not here for polite conversation, have you come merely to gloat?'

Jasper sat on the ground opposite Twm and pulled the scarf from his face, he began to speak in the English tongue.

'I believe that you are a good friend of Richard Cadwgan,' he said.

'Our families have been friends for many years,' said Twm carefully.

'He has a lass about your age,' continued Jasper. Twm stiffened, but he hid his feelings as the man continued.

'I need a new kitchen maid,' he hesitated, 'but Cadwgan is no friend of mine and has refused to help me many times. If you can find a way to bring Cadwgan's lass to me I will set you free.'

Twm pretended to ponder for a while. He didn't trust Jasper an inch, and knew that the man was not particularly kind to his servants. He was always looking for young girls to work for him, but often they were taken to his house never to be seen again. The villagers said that they were taken to some place far away, but no-one knew where. Twm did not wish to see his friend Gwenni brought to this man. However, he kept his own counsel, and waited for Jasper to continue.

'Bring Cadwgan's lass to you,' Twm repeated responding to Jasper in English. Jasper's eyes glistened.

'Aye,' he replied, 'either that or you hang tomorrow.'

'And my friends with me, no doubt,' said Twm.

'If you mean the crowd involved in that pagan Mari Lwyd thing, they deserve such punishment,' retorted Jasper angrily.

'Well, well,' said Twm, his voice was placatory. 'Even if I could do this thing for you, I would think that her father would immediately come after her.'

'No, he couldn't,' said Jasper, excitedly, 'I intend to employ her at some property I have far away from here, Cadwgan will never find her again.'

Twm was more and more convinced that Jasper intended harm to young Gwenni, but he wanted to hear more, a plan was beginning to form in his head.

'Where exactly do you want me to bring the lass?'

Jasper tried to sound calm again, 'I want her brought round to the back of the house and taken up the stairs to a small room at the top of the house. I will arrange for her to be taken from there to my other property. Most of the servants at the Hall are having a party in town so there will be few to interfere with you.'

Twm appeared to consider Jasper's proposal. He was now quite angry but his voice was icy calm. 'You know that if there was a whisper that I had helped you in this way, my life would be in danger from Gwenni's father, Richard Cadwgan and his friends, and I couldn't blame them.'

'That is for you to deal with,' said Jasper indifferently, 'I don't doubt you will think of something, you always do.'

'That is true,' said Twm gravely, but his eyes danced for a moment. He appeared to be considering Jasper's proposal. Finally he rose to his feet. Jasper also stood up waiting for Twm's answer.

'If I do this thing,' he said, 'you will have to promise to let my friends go free as well. Their freedom may mitigate my own part in this matter. And you must also settle matters with Elias.'

'It is a bargain,' said Jasper 'here's my hand on it.' Twm appeared not to notice Jasper's proffered hand. With a great show of reluctance, Twm said, 'Since I seem to have little choice, I agree.'

Jasper Tyler with a small out take of breath, said briskly, 'Good. I want you to bring Cadwgan's lass to me tomorrow at midnight.'

Jasper went to the door of the cell and called out to the jailer.

'Jailer, come here at once.' Elphin appeared and waited for instructions.

'Do you know who I am?' asked Jasper.

'I didn't know when you came in Sir,' replied Elphin, 'but now I can see your face I recognise you. You are Jasper Tyler, Justice of the Peace.'

'You appear to be responsible man,' said the Squire who was slightly mollified by Elphin's respectful demeanour.

'Now,' he continued, pompously, 'I want you to release this man. I came here to examine him in my capacity as Justice of the Peace. I am a fair man.' Elphin hid a wry smile of disbelief. Jasper continued, 'Before making a decision which would cost a man his life, I wanted to see if he showed a proper repentance for his misdemeanours. I am satisfied that a night in jail has taught him a lesson. I think he should now be released. If he stays here until morning, I doubt whether the hangman sent by the English will show such mercy.'

'Certainly Sir, and may I say sir, with the

greatest humility that I applaud your sense of justice and mercy.' Elphin knew how to flatter the man who employed him.

'What do I do about the others?' he went on, deferentially. 'Are you leaving them to the hangman?' Seeing the determined look on Twm's face, Jasper replied, 'Oh! let them all go as well, I understand that they were only taking part in the Mari Lwyd party and we all know that she brings good luck!'

Elphin looked at Twm, astounded at the Squire's hypocrisy, but Twm's face was impassive.

'Right sir,' said Elphin, 'and may I say, that your own kindness will undoubtedly be rewarded by the Mari Lwyd.' Jasper looked at the jailer trying to detect some double meaning behind his words, but the jailer's face was as innocent as the day.

So Twm followed Jasper out of the jail and into the night. Elphin's keys could be heard turning in the locks of the other cells.

'Out you go my friends, and you can thank the Squire for your freedom,' he lowered his voice and whispered, 'and Twm Siôn Cati.'

Outside the jail, Twm and Jasper parted. The Squire rode back to his house and Twm walked jauntily in the opposite direction towards Fountain Gate.

CADWGAN'S ASS

TWM SLEPT that night in his own home. The following morning, he rode round to see his friend Richard Cadwgan, who lived on the outskirts of the town. He owned a small holding including two geese and a gander, six hens, a small pony and an ass called Betsy.

Cadwgan was scattering corn to the hens.

'Hello Richard,' said Twm, as he dismounted and tied his pony, Cothi, to a tree.

'Hello Twm,' replied Richard. 'I thought you were in jail.'

'It takes a lot to keep me tied up,' grinned Twm.

'How is Betsy?' he asked, patting her on the back as he spoke.

'Fine,' said Richard. 'Why?'

'I wondered if I could borrow her for a while,' said Twm.

'What are you up to now?' asked Richard.

'Well, up to no good as you can guess,' laughed Twm, 'but it will only cause trouble to people we don't like.'

'That's good enough for me,' said Richard. 'Borrow her with pleasure.'

'I'll bring her back safe and sound, don't worry,' said Twm.

'I'm sure you will,' laughed Richard 'and I don't want to know what you want her for.'

Twm led Betsy out of Richard Cadwgan's field to where he had tied up Cothi. He jumped on the horse's back and took hold of the rope around the ass's neck.

'Come on my beauty,' he said, 'you have work to do.'

The ass docilely trotted along behind Cothi, back to Fountain Gate. She and the pony were good friends and often played together in Richard Cadwgan's field. When Twm had tethered Betsy in the field behind the house he gave her some food and water and left her there until it grew dark.

That night, if anyone had been watching, they would have seen the shadowy figure of Twm leading Betsy along the road towards the Big House owned by Jasper Tyler. Jasper employed many servants in the house and on his large farm. Most of these servants lived in Tregaron or in the small villages nearby.

Twm led Betsy to the back of the house, and pulled some clothes out of a big bag he had slung over the ass's back. He began to cover Betsy's back with a flowered cotton dress, which belonged to his mother, Cati, and pulled a flowery cap on her head! Betsy stamped up and down, not liking the treatment she was getting from Twm, but he quickly gave her an apple which he had covered with honey. She loved apples and she loved honey so she forgot about the clothes and munched contentedly at the fruit.

Twm caught hold of the reins and pulled Betsy through the back door and pushed her from behind up the back stairs. Twm had a way with animals and he talked persuasively to Betsy coaxing her all the way up the stairs until they reached the room Jasper had described to Twm.

Jasper was hiding along the corridor and heard the clatter as Betsy and Twm climbed the stairs.

'Twm must be having some trouble with the girl,' thought Jasper, 'she's not coming willingly.'

Twm pushed Betsy into the room. Then he set

down in front of her a basket of fruit and some water which he knew would make her happy. What she didn't know was that Twm had put something in the food to make her more docile! He waited until Betsy quietened down, then he threw a large quilt from the bed over her and quietly made his escape. But he didn't move too far away, he wanted to watch the fun!

Jasper was also waiting until all was quiet. When silence seemed to descend on the room where Twm had put Betsy, Jasper thought to himself, 'I expect that Twm has persuaded the girl that she will be safely looked after by my housekeeper Mary, and is probably settling down for the night.'

He opened the door and moved quietly into the room. When his eyes became accustomed to the darkness he could see a heap on the floor. It looked like a body covered by the bed quilt! Jasper had a rope ready in his hand to tie up the girl. He crept closer to the heap on the floor then suddenly snatched the quilt away. As he did so, the startled ass jumped up and began kicking and jumping all over the room, hee-hawing loudly. Jasper took fright and tried to get away.

He tumbled out of the room and stumbled down the stairs with the ass in pursuit. Finally they both landed on the bottom of the stairs with the ass on top of Jasper Tyler.

Jasper struggled to pull himself from underneath the ass, and managed to get to his feet, dishevelled and bruised. He was livid with anger, and glared at the crowd who had gathered at the bottom of the stairs. Jasper's servants had returned from their night out and had heard the commotion. Among them he could see Twm looking anxious and solicitous.

'Are you alright, sir?' asked Twm innocently, he spoke very deliberately in English. Jasper did not want to look foolish in front of his servants and swallowed his anger.

'Where did this creature come from?' He roared. 'I heard some movement in the servant's quarters and went to investigate. I thought we had thieves breaking in to the house, instead I found this ridiculous creature in one of the servant's rooms!'

'I do apologise sir,' said Twm sweetly, 'you know that you recently asked me to bring Cadwgan's *ass* secretly to the servant's quarters,' Twm emphasised the word *ass*. 'I thought you were playing a pleasant trick on your servants since you said that they would be away tonight.' Jasper's face looked apoplectic.

'Don't you remember?' Twm continued sweetly. 'You came to see me in jail a few nights ago? You were kind enough to tell the jailer to set me free, and my friends because you wanted to save us from the English hangman. Such a just and merciful man!' Twm turned round so that Jasper could not see his face. He was holding his sides with laughter.

Jasper Tyler was so angry he could not speak. He stood up, turned on his heel and stalked into the house. The servants looked after him.

'This is a sorry day for you, Twm' said Meirion, 'You have made such a fool of him, he is bound to plan a dreadful revenge. I wouldn't like to be in your shoes.'

'He will have to find me first,' said Twm carelessly.

TWM IN DANGER

TWM WAS OFTEN away from home for days at a time, living in the countryside around Tregaron, no-one knew where he was, but he slept comfortably in the cave he had discovered on the hillside away from prying eyes. Now he was hiding in his cave, away from Jasper's anger and retribution. He knew that the squire would never forgive him for making him look ridiculous in front of his servants, so he had to lie low, thinking of a way out of his predicament. When he lay in his cave at night before going to sleep, he sometimes thought about his father. He remembered one day in particular when he was about seven years old. He and Cati were in the garden. Cati sat on the swing, he sprawled on the ground by her side.

'Where is my father?' said Twm suddenly. Cati stopped swinging. She became very still.

'What made you think of that?' she asked.

'Oh, I don't know,' said Twm carelessly. 'Watt was having a scrap with his father this morning, they were just playing and having fun. I thought, 'I couldn't do that with Tad-cu, because he is too old. And then I thought that it would be nice to play like that with my father and I began wondering where he was. I thought perhaps he may have died and you didn't want to tell me.'

'He isn't dead,' she said quietly. 'He lives in a big house in Dinefwr and he is very rich.' Twm was shocked.

'Then why don't we live with him?' he asked. Cati smiled at her son.

'You may be a bit too young to understand,' she said. 'When you were born, he asked me to go with him to live in Dinefwr, but I refused. I didn't want to live far away from all my friends. So he gave me this house instead. I've been happy here Twm, haven't you?'

'Yes of course, Mam,' said Twm. He was silent again. 'But who is he?' he persisted.

'He comes from the family of Moetheu,' said Cati somewhat evasively. 'His first name is David. He has other names but I will tell you more about him when you are older.'

'But doesn't he want to see me?' asked Twm sadly.

'Oh, yes,' said Cati, 'and I let him know how you are, but he thinks it best to leave you alone to enjoy your life with me and your friends in Tregaron. I don't think you want to know any more,' she said as she saw her son about to ask another question. 'Always remember that we both love you very much.'

Twm knew from the tone of his mother's voice that it was better not to persist with his questions, but his face closed up and he looked very sad.

Cati watched him and her face softened, 'You can be very proud of your family Twm. Tad-cu is related to the great Herbert family.' Twm's eyes grew very large and round. Cati continued, 'And he tells me that he is even distantly related to Henry Tudor, the King of England! So always remember that you have noble blood in your veins from *both* sides of your family!

Twm kept his mother's words close in his heart.

But now while he hid in his cave in Dinas, wondering how he was to escape the law of Jasper

Tyler, he wondered why he had been thinking about that conversation with his mother. Maybe it had something to do with his concern over Jasper Tyler's interest in Gwenni. They had been good friends ever since their schooldays. Twm thought of the Squire's anger at the way he had made him look ridiculous in front of his servants. Jasper Tyler was certain to attempt some horrible revenge on Twm Siôn Cati.

Twm's sober meditations were interrupted by a soft whistle from outside the cave. It was the signal he had arranged with Watt. He gave a whistle in response and soon Watt's head appeared beneath him. His friend scrambled up into the cave and flung himself down by the side of Twm. Twm waited until Watt had regained his breath.

'Well old friend,' he said, 'how are things at home?'

'Worse than you could ever imagine,' said Watt grimly. 'Jasper has arrested Richard Cadwgan and taken Gwenni away!' Twm's face changed colour.

'Where has he taken her?' he asked.

'No-one knows,' said Watt, 'but there are rumours that he has locked her up in one of his properties over in Carmarthen. I'm sure that no-one will ever be able to find her again.' Watt's voice choked with emotion.

'I will kill him,' Twm said. His voice was icy cold.

'Don't be a fool,' said his friend, 'you are only one. He has many men to protect him and he has the power of the English throne behind him!'

'The law of England and Mary, the Queen of England,' said Twm scornfully, 'their laws are not for the likes of us.' He stopped and went quite quiet. Finally he said in a very measured tone, 'I will never rest until Jasper Tyler pays for what he has done to Richard and to Gwenni.' He stood up resolutely, 'I swear by all that I hold dear, that I will never return to Tregaron until I have made sure that that man has got his just deserts. I will search for Gwenni, and if I cannot save her, I will avenge her and her family with all the power and skill that I possess.' He held out his hand to his friend.

'Join me Watt,' he smiled, 'we will become the most feared outlaws in the country.' Watt clasped Twm's hand, 'I can't Twm, I must go on living in

Tregaron, your mother is able to support herself, but my family are poor, they depend on me for their livelihood.' He looked at Twm's solemn face. 'But I will join you whenever I can old friend, and I will keep you informed of Jasper's movements.'

So the two friends shook hands and embraced. Then Watt slipped out of the cave and left Twm to a new and dangerous life. As long as Jasper Tyler was alive, Twm would live the life of a outlaw and never again be able to return openly to visit his friends and family in Tregaron.

TWM REPRIEVED

SO TWM SIÔN CATI lived in the countryside near his cave, when the sun shone, and sought shelter in solitary taverns along the bye-roads during the harsher weather. He survived for the few years that Queen Mary ruled England, by living the life of an outlaw. He robbed from rich squires like Jasper Tyler and shopkeepers like Elias Richards when he found them riding along the roads and tracks and byways of Wales. He often shared his new found wealth with the poor folk he found begging along the roadside or outside the taverns, so ordinary folk frequently sheltered him from the prying eyes of Jasper's spies. To hide his identity, when he held up the rich travellers, he sometimes used one of the masks he had taken with him from the old box in his mother's house, Fountain Gate. His favourite mask was made in the likeness of a hawk.

Occasionally, he rode to London, on his beloved pony, Cothi. Indeed it was at a London market that he had assumed the guise of a Welsh drover and sold the prize bull he and Watt had stolen from Jasper. It was easy for Twm to live in London undetected, because the city at that time was a city in turmoil under the reign of Queen Mary. She hated her father, King Henry VIII so much, that when she became queen she gave orders to imprison and put to death anyone known to have sympathised with Henry's old regime. In this climate of fear, London was a place of danger, frequented by travellers, vagabonds, outlaws, thieves and merchants.

Twm Siôn Cati lived in this wild and dangerous way for some time, until finally, Queen Mary died and Elizabeth succeeded her sister to the throne of England. A year later, he heard the familiar whistle which signalled that his friend Watt was at hand with the news of the day. He greeted his friend warmly.

'Sit down and share a meal with me,' said Twm, turning a rabbit over on the spit in front of him.

'Thank you Twm,' said Watt, 'but I have come with great news.' Twm left the rabbit on the spit, and looked up at his friend.

'Queen Elizabeth has announced an amnesty for everyone who has committed any crimes since Mary came to the throne.' Watt was so excited he blurted out the news at once, his eyes shining.

'I can't see how that applies to me,' said Twm dourly, 'It is English law, she means it for her own people.'

'No! No!' said Watt. 'It is said that she believes that all the land over which she rules, which includes Wales, has suffered under her 'cousin' as she calls her, Queen Mary. There was no love lost between them as you know, although King Henry was father to them both. Elizabeth has said that she wishes to heal wounds and create peace and harmony.'

'Watt, this may be true, and I can hardly believe it, indeed I won't believe it until I see some real evidence that this pardon applies to me.'

'Come with me to Tregaron,' urged Watt. 'Jasper Tyler fled after Queen Mary died, he was no longer in favour with Elizabeth's men. He has been replaced by Richard.'

'Richard,' said Twm in disbelief, 'Richard Cadwgan.'

'Yes,' said Watt excitedly, 'and Gwenni's back. They found her in Jasper's house in Carmarthen. She had been locked up for most of the time as we guessed, but she had come to no further harm. She is home, but she is changed, quieter than you remember her.'

Twm waited no longer, he flung himself on to his horse, Watt jumped up behind him and they both rode at a gallop to Tregaron.

When they arrived at the Great Hall, which once belonged to Jasper Tyler, it was all as Watt had said. Richard Cadwgan greeted Twm Siôn Cati affectionately.

'Well my friend,' he said, smiling, 'so times have changed!'

'Very much,' laughed Twm, 'I still can't believe it.'

'Let me show you the Great Seal,' said Richard, 'then you can no longer doubt your good fortune.'

So Richard led Twm into the library of the Big House and brought out the parchment scroll from his desk.

'Here you are Twm,' he said. Twm took the

scroll, and read the Latin. Watt leaning over his shoulder, said,

'Read it in our own tongue Twm, let us all hear it.'

Twm said slowly,

'Queen Elizabeth forgives Twm Siôn Cati, alias Thomas Jones, for all misdemeanours perpetrated during the reign of her cousin, Mary.'

His face broke into a grin, he looked at his old friends and then at the great red seal attached to the parchment he held in his hand. He was no longer in any doubt that he was at last a free man. The whole village rejoiced at Twm Siôn Cati's reprieve and there was much dancing and singing and feasting in the village of Tregaron.

Afterwards Thomas Jones took up residence in Fountain Gate and became one of the most respected country squires in Wales. He no longer used his former name of Twm Siôn Cati, and proudly proclaimed his noble heritage by creating his own family coat of arms. Many other noble families asked him to do the same for them and he became known as the greatest heraldic bard in all the country.

But he will be better remembered in Wales as the outlaw who remained defiant of the powerful and corrupt people who suppressed the poor in the wild and dangerous times of Twm Siôn Cati.